This igloo book belongs to:

....

igloobooks

Published in 2020
First published in the UK by Igloo Books Ltd
An imprint of Igloo Books Ltd
Cottage Farm, NN6 0BJ, UK
Owned by Bonnier Books
Sveavägen 56, Stockholm, Sweden
www.igloobooks.com

1020 003
2 4 6 8 10 9 7 5 3
ISBN 978-1-83852-218-6

Written by Stephanie Moss
Illustrated by Leire Martín

Designed by Justine Ablett
Edited by Stephanie Moss

Printed and manufactured in China

The TALLEST HOUSE on the STREET

igloobooks

One day, Giraffe appeared in her too-small moving van.
She needed a new house and she had come here with a plan.

"I must have something tall," she said,
"that fits my neck just right."

This time she
wanted housemates
who were fun,
kind and polite.

NEW RD.

FRESH ST.

HAPPY END

No more living on her own.
Those days were finished,

DONE!

Goodbye to lonely parties
where the guest was only one.

So she knocked,

Tap-Tap

on Horse's door.

He answered with a grin.

"I'm looking for a house," she said. So Horse replied,

Come in!

His stables were so elegant.
He'd painted them bright blue.

"I love it," said Giraffe, "but my long neck just goes straight through!"

So she knocked,
Tap-Tap
on Hippo's door.

He answered straight away.

"I'm looking for a house,"
she said. So Hippo called,

Hooray!

SNACK SHACK

MUD BATH

HOT TUB

His house was one big waterhole. He jumped and yelled, "Woo-hoo!"
"I love it," said Giraffe, "but I'm too tall to play with you."

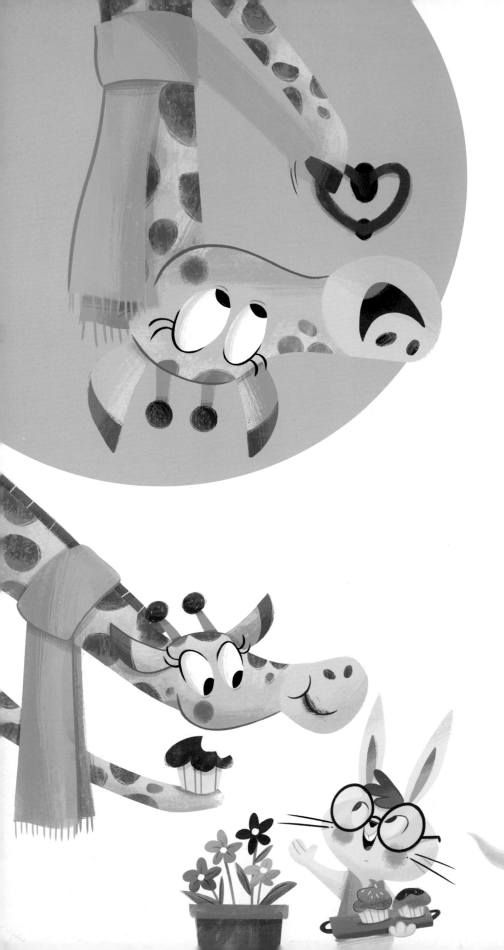

So she knocked,

Tap-Tap

on Bunny's door.

He answered, smiling bright.

"I'm looking for a house," she said. So Bunny said,

Alright!

The burrow looked so cosy. She could hardly ask for more.
"I love it," said Giraffe, "but I just can't fit through the door!"

HOME *sweet* HOME

Giraffe couldn't give up yet,
for her search had just begun.
"I know just how to help," said Mouse.
"Now let's go have some fun!"

Mouse showed her places long enough, but sadly they weren't tall.

Another one was closer by,
but wouldn't fit at all!

"I've got a big, tall windmill, with a lovely meadow view.

But if you want your friends close by, it might not be for you."

They saw all kinds of homes that
towered high up off the ground.
But just like her old houses,
no one lived for miles around.

4A Long Beach Ride

17 Faraway Avenue

28 Sky-high Views

1 Lonely Place

12 Chimes Road

3 Birds Nest Close

"I'll take one," sighed Giraffe,
and then she reached down for the key.

"It seems like a house far away
is all there is for me."

She drove off far away again, in her small moving van.
But little did she know, this time her friends had hatched a plan.

Giraffe started unpacking, as they all worked day and night
to build a house on their own street that would fit her just right.

They knocked,

Tap-Tap

on Giraffe's door.
She answered with a grin.

"We've built you
a house," they said.

And we're all moving in!"

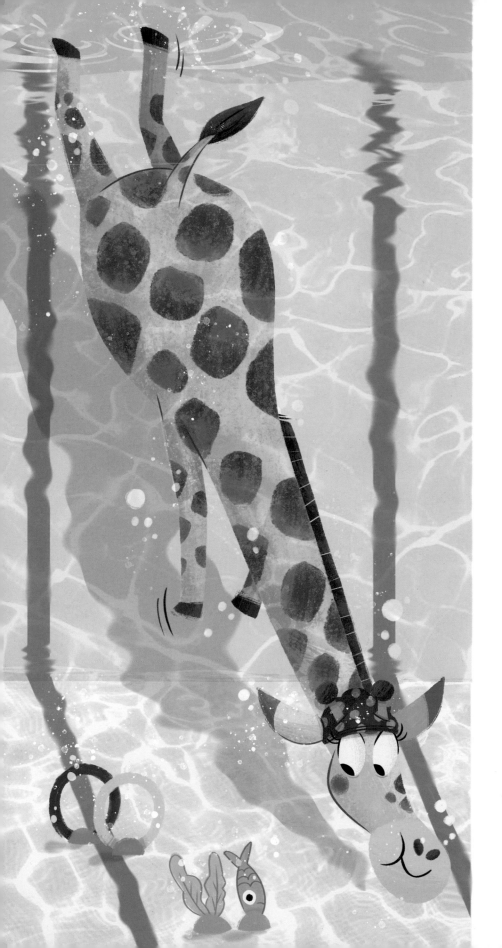

It had a great big waterhole.
The walls were all bright blue.
It was super cosy...
and she fit **perfectly**, too.
But the **best** part of all was
something none of that could beat.

Her friends made room for her with the **TALLEST** house on the street.